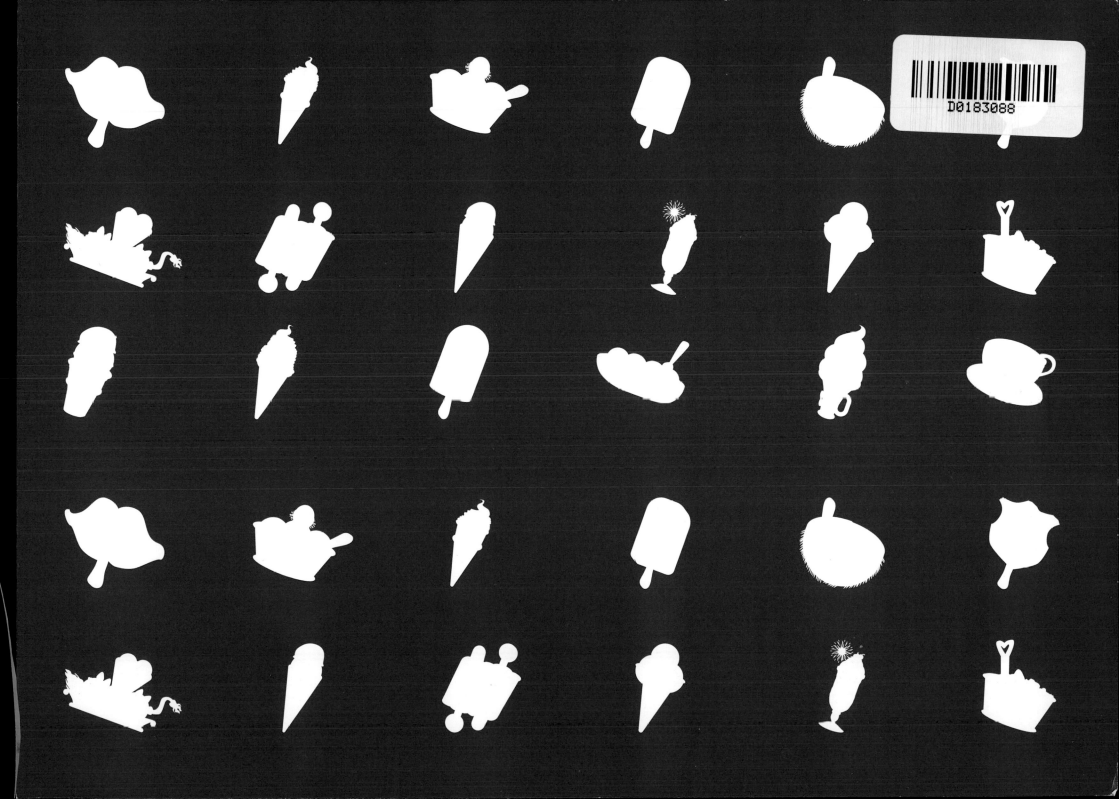

This book is dedicated to Conor (with one n), our number one fan. Thank you for your support, from one author to another.

With thanks to Milly Clark, inventor of 'Mama Mia Mango!' gelato, our 'Pick a Flavour' competition winner.

First published in 2018 by Dacima Books Ltd.
Orbital House, 20 Eastern Road, Romford, Essex, RM1 3PJ.

www.dacimabooks.com

ISBN 978 1 9996208 4 4 (Hard back)
ISBN 978 1 9996208 3 7 (Paper back)
ISBN 978 1 9996208 5 1 (eBook)

The Gelato King

Book Two of the

City of Justice Trilogy

Words by Dionne Paull, pictures by Corey Harris

dacima books

Luigi the Gelato King was someone quite unique:
Even through the winter months he dressed in summer chic.

Known throughout the city for his most exquisite taste,
Each morning he would tie a silken apron 'round his waist.

The letters 'G' and 'K' were inscribed with velvet string;
Standing for his sobriquet, the city's "Gelato King".

Choosing what to wear was quite the complication:
To create an ensemble from his colourful collection

Of Hawaiian shirts, fancy hats, and Bermuda-printed shorts,
His gigantic walk-in wardrobe was full of vibrant sorts.

Stagionale

~ Apples ~
~ Brussel Sprouts ~
~ Clementines ~
~ Kiwi Fruit ~
~ Lemons ~
~ Oranges ~
~ Passion Fruit ~
~ Pears ~
~ Pomegranates ~
Raspberry
~ Strawberry ~
~ Tonka Bean ~

Locale

~ Carrots ~
~ Cherries ~
~ Chom Chom ~
~ Cranberry ~
~ Dragon Fruit ~
~ Ginger ~
~ Hazelnuts ~
Pistachio
~ Radish ~
~ Rhubarb ~
~ Star Anise ~
~ Vanilla Bean ~

20 kilograms fresh raspberries

He sold his ice-creams daily, and made them through the night;
His cellar was a factory of sumptuous delights.

His flavours made him famous ~ they simply were divine.
The lunch queue stretched and snaked around the city in a line.

But one hot summer's day his world came crashing down;
It began when a patron licked his cornet with a frown.

"Is there a problem, Sir?" Luigi said, feeling sad.
"Yes," replied the man. "This ice-cream's really bad.

The colour red is right: I ordered sorbet melon.
But the taste has curled my toes ~ it's sour bitter lemon."

"Let me taste it," said Gelato King, and took a mighty lick.
Luigi froze with fright, in fact he felt quite sick.

Then he gasped in horror as another lady said,
"This is not white chocolate, it tastes like gingerbread."

Luigi tested all his flavours, sampling one by one.
"The ingredients are mixed up!" he cried "Oh no, what have I done?"

He slumped down to his knees with head held in his hands,
When at this desperate moment heard a voice behind his van.

"Luigi, my good fellow, you have customers in line,"
Said the spy of the city, arriving in perfect time.

"Oh Spy, you must help me, my flavours are all jumbled ~
Vanilla's white in colour, but tastes like apple crumble!

I can't think how this happened, my method is precise.
I'll need to shut my business ~ but ice-cream is my life!"

"A job for me!" said Spy. "It doesn't make much sense.
I have an itchy feeling it's a criminal offence."

He helped Luigi to his feet and whispered in his ear,
"We need to be on high alert, I think the culprit's near."

"Culprit?" asked Luigi. "Who'd spoil my gelato?"
But Spy had spotted someone dressed up incognito.

"Look," said Spy, "at that suspicious woman over there ~
She wears a coat and boots, and her hat hides all her hair.

It's the middle of the summer and today is very hot.
She's in disguise or hiding something ~ and we must find out what!

Distract your clientele: give cornets out for free.
I'll sneak around the queue ~ no one will notice me."

The spy was skilled and smooth, unseen by all around:
He crawled and rolled and tiptoed ~ and never made a sound.

He sneaked up on his target, reached out and grabbed her arm ~
But what was this he felt? A hairy wrist was in his palm.

News Stand

J.C.N
NEWS
with
VIEWS

Dash and Grab!

...and, Tree!

...Slip Quietly...

...Saunter Casually...

Crawl...

...Snip and Read Manoeuvre...

...Scramble...

...Duck!

...and now!

Tip...

Toe...

...Shuffle...

...Roll...

"You're no woman!" Spy yelled. "You're a man in disguise."
He searched the suspect's overcoat, and revealed a big surprise!

Tubes of different colours were all lined up inside ~
A diversity of shades, with a label saying "Dyes".

"Show your face," demanded Spy, "before I handcuff you!"
The man took off his hat to expose... Luigi, number two?

"My name is Lorenzo. I surrender to you, Spy.
Luigi's my twin brother." He then began to cry.

"Luigi," shouted Spy, "come over here at once."
"I'm sorry," sobbed Lorenzo. "I've always felt a dunce.

Luigi, you're the clever one, determined, full of energy.
I struggled to keep up with you, and now look what's become of me."

"Lorenzo, my twin brother, you switched my flavours all around.
You could have ruined my business. Strawberry's now brown!"

"Please forgive me, my good brother, I'm jealous and a fool.
Take me off to prison, Spy: I deserve it ~ I've been so cruel."

Luigi grabbed Lorenzo and hugged his brother tight.
"Come with me, Lorenzo ~ everything will be alright.

Families must stick together through good times and the bad.
Talk to me, be honest ~ don't stay alone and sad."

"You're so busy," said Lorenzo, "you don't have time for me."
"You're right," admitted Luigi. "I do work constantly.

I must focus on what's important and find time for us two.
Why don't you be my partner? I can spend each day with you!"

The offer was accepted; they're now the Gelato Twins!
They don't have crowns like royalty, but with love they feel like kings.

The Gelato Twins' Gelataria

Bacio

Cake-on-a-Cone

Chom~Chom Nom~Nom

Dragon Fruit Surprise

Higgledy Piggledy Pop

Hokey~Pokey

Mint Choc-Chip

Rainbow Ripple

Raspberry Nojito

Coconut Crunch

Cool Cucumber

The C.O.J

Kiwi Kurse

Mama Mia Mango!

Merry Berries

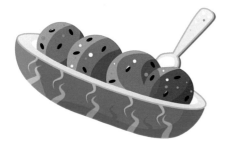

Sorbet Melon

Tooty Fruity

White Choca Mocha

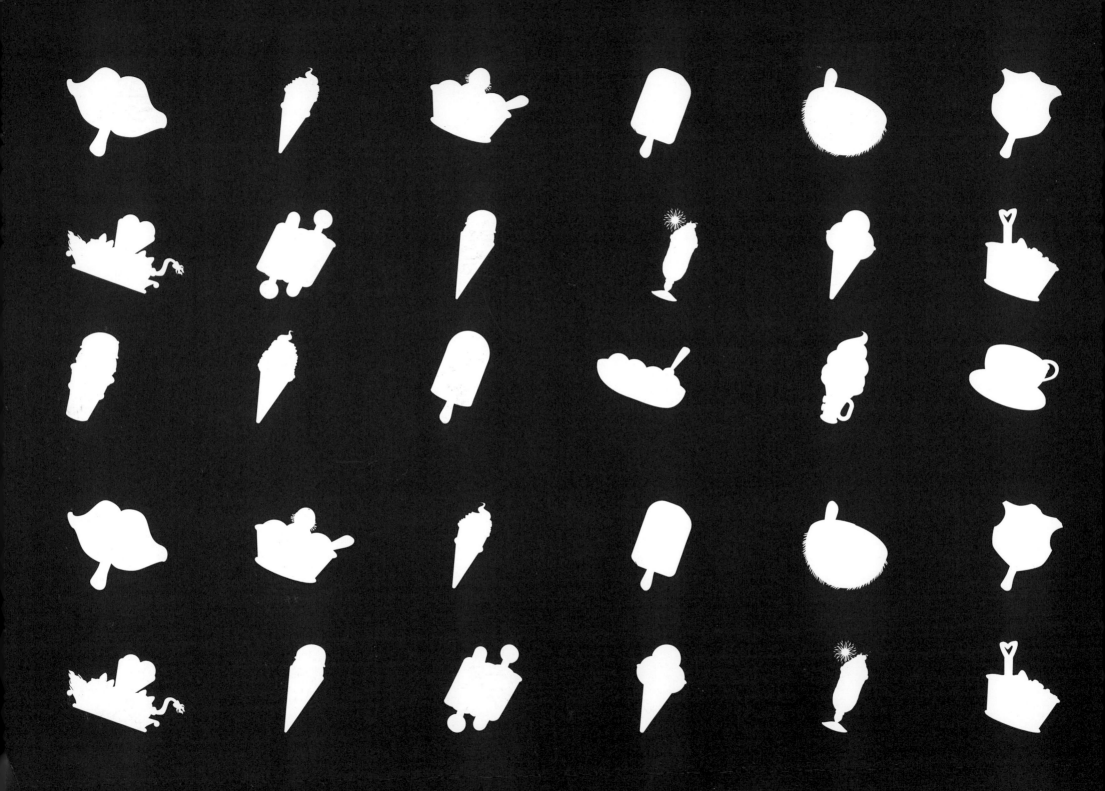